WARREN

Bunnykins in the Snow

Illustrated by

Walter Hayward

Viking Kestrel

ALSO BY WARRENER

A Picnic for Bunnykins
Two Bunnykins out to Tea
Bunnykins in the Kitchen

VIKING KESTREL
Penguin Books Ltd, Harmondsworth, Middlesex, England
Viking Penguin Inc., 40 West 23rd Street, New York, New York 10010, U.S.A.
Penguin Books Australia Ltd, Ringwood, Victoria, Australia
Penguin Books Canada Ltd, 2801 John Street, Markham, Ontario, Canada L3R 1B4
Penguin Books (N.Z.) Ltd, 182–190 Wairau Road, Auckland 10, New Zealand

First published 1985
Text copyright © Warrener, 1985
Illustrations copyright © Royal Doulton (UK) Ltd, 1985
Bunnykins® is a registered trademark of Doulton & Co. Ltd

Library of Congress catalog card number:
British Library Cataloguing in Publication Data

Warrener
Bunnykins in the snow.
I. Title
823′.914[J]   PZ7

ISBN 0-670-80568-8

Printed in Great Britain

The rabbit characters from which the now traditional
Bunnykins® image evolved were created by an English
nun. Royal Doulton discovered her pencil drawings
in the 1930s and transformed them into the colourful
tableware and figures that have delighted
generations of children ever since.

Royal Doulton's own artists have continued the theme
and today designer Walter Hayward is responsible for
creating new scenes, each telling its own story with
an ageless charm and artistry, for use on their range
of gift pottery cherished by children the world over.

Once upon a bunnytime,
in winter, the Bunnykins family
looked out and saw that it was snowing.
It snowed and snowed and snowed.
At last it stopped.
Then Mrs Bunnykins said:
'Now you can play outside
in the snow!'

Out rushed all the little Bunnykins
into the deep snow.
They ran in it and kicked in it
and jumped in it and danced in it.

With their paws they scooped it
and scattered it and flung it all about.

They made snowballs and threw them
and began a great snow-battle.

In the middle of the battle,
Mrs Bunnykins came out to them,
carrying a tray with six white mugs on it
and one little yellow one.

The mugs were steaming
in the frosty air, because each mug
had a hot drink inside it.
Mrs Bunnykins knew exactly
which hot drink each of her
children liked best.

There was a mug of hot tea for one little
Bunnykins.

There was a mug of hot coffee for
another little Bunnykins.

There was a mug of hot chocolate for
another little Bunnykins.

There was a mug of hot milk for
another little Bunnykins.

There was a mug of hot orange
for another little Bunnykins.
There was a mug of hot water
– yes! just hot water –
for another little Bunnykins.

There was a mug of hot soup
for the last little Bunnykins, the littlest.
His name was Bunting.
He liked soup made from carrots,
and he liked to drink his carrot soup
from his own little yellow mug.

The little Bunnykins stopped their
snow-battle and drank their hot drinks.
Then they put their empty mugs
down on the ground, and said:
'Let's make a snow-bunny!'

Each little Bunnykins made
a roly-poly snowball as big as possible.
Then the roly-poly snowballs
were all piled one on top of each other,
to make the tall body of the snow-bunny.
The smallest, roundest snowball
went right on top to make
the snow-bunny's head.

It was too difficult to make
long snow-ears for the snow-bunny;
so they borrowed an old hat
from their father
to put on the snow-bunny's head
and to cover up where the snow-ears
should have been.

They also borrowed an old pipe
to stick in the snow-bunny's mouth.
They put a black pebble
for the snow-bunny's nose
and two black pebbles for his eyes.

They had just finished their snow-bunny
when their mother came out
to call them indoors:
it was nearly bedtime.
When she saw them, she cried:
'Oh dear! You're covered in snow!
You can't bring all that snow
into the house! As you come in,
you must all take off your clothes
and leave them with me,
and go upstairs to the bathroom
to have a hot bath.'

So the little Bunnykins
all took off their snowy clothes at the door
and then went inside in nothing but
brown fur and little white tails.
But they didn't go straight
to the bathroom
– they were too excited for that.

When they were free of all their clothes,
they began to run

– they ran and they ran and they ran.

They ran upstairs and downstairs

and through doorways and round corners
and under tables and over chairs

– they ran and they ran and they ran.

They ran WILD, as only bunnies can.

   While they were running,
Mrs Bunnykins shook the snow
from their clothes and
hung them up to dry.
And she asked her husband
to bring indoors the seven empty mugs
left out in the snow.

Mr Bunnykins went outside and found
the mug for tea and the mug for coffee

and the mug for chocolate

and the mug for milk

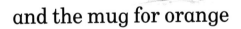

and the mug for orange

and the mug for water;

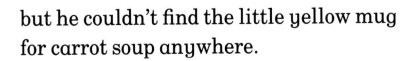

but he couldn't find the little yellow mug
for carrot soup anywhere.

He searched all round the snow-bunny
and where the snow-battle had been.
He searched everywhere,
but he could *not* find
the little yellow mug.
    So Mr Bunnykins
took the six mugs indoors,
and washed them up, and dried them,
and hung them on their hooks.

Then he went upstairs to the bathroom,
where the little Bunnykins were having
a hot bath, helped by their mother.
Sadly he told Bunting
that his little yellow mug was lost.

Bunting began to cry.

His mother said: 'Don't cry, Bunting.
Your yellow mug is sure
to turn up again one day.'

His father said: 'Until it does turn up,
you can share my big white mug
at breakfast and dinner and tea.'

So Bunting cheered up a little.
He shared his father's big white mug
at breakfast and dinner and tea
the next day and the next day
and the next day after that.

During those three days,
it didn't snow any more,
and the sun shone.
The sun shone quite warmly.
It melted the snow on the ground,
and it began to melt the snow-bunny.

On the first day the sun shone,
the snow-bunny was just a little shorter
and a little thinner
and his pipe fell out of his mouth.

On the second day the sun shone,
he was a lot shorter
and a lot thinner
and his hat fell off.

On the third day the sun shone,
he was so short and thin
that he was hardly there at all,
and his pebble eyes
and his pebble nose had gone.
He was really just
a little heap of melting snow.

All the Bunnykins family
came out to look
at what was left of the snow-bunny.
    Suddenly Bunting said:
'What's that poking up
out of the heap of snow? It's yellow,
and – Why! It looks just like
my little yellow mug that was lost!'

And so it was.

The Bunnykins children had built their snow-bunny right on top of Bunting's yellow mug, without noticing!

That evening Bunting had hot carrot soup out of his little yellow mug again. He was very happy.

And that is the end of this bunnytale.